Along Came A **Different**

BLOOMSBURY

For the Donalds of this world.

BLOOMSBURY CHILDREN'S BOOKS
Bloomsbury Publishing Plc
50 Bedford Square, London, WC1B 3DP, UK

BLOOMSBURY, BLOOMSBURY CHILDREN'S BOOKS and the Diana logo are
trademarks of Bloomsbury Publishing Plc
First published in Great Britain 2018 by Bloomsbury Publishing Plc
This edition published in Great Britain 2019 by Bloomsbury Publishing Plc

A catalogue record for this book is available from the British Library

ISBN: HB: 978 1 4088 8892 6; PB: 978 1 4088 8894 0; eBook: 978 1 4088 8893 3

1 3 5 7 9 10 8 6 4 2

Printed and bound in China by Leo

All papers used by Bloomsbury Publishing Plc are natural,
recyclable products from wood grown in well managed forests.
The manufacturing processes conform to the environmental regulations of the country of origin.

To find out more about our authors and books visit
www.bloomsbury.com and sign up for our newsletters

Along Came A **Different**

Tom McLaughlin

BLOOMSBURY
CHILDREN'S BOOKS

LONDON OXFORD NEW YORK NEW DELHI SYDNEY

The Reds loved being red.

They wore **red hats,** sang **red songs** and ate **red apples.**

And they all agreed that being a **Red** was The. Best. Thing. Ever.

Then one day, quite unexpectedly . . .

along came a different.

The Yellows loved being **yellow.**

They ate **yellow bananas,** read **yellow books**

and drove **yellow cars.**

And *they* all agreed that being a **Yellow** was The. Best. Thing. Ever.

The problem was . . .

the Yellows didn't like **the Reds.**

They thought their

red apples

were **too round,**

their **red hats** were **too pointy**

and their **red music**
was much too loud.

And so . . .

this happened!

along came **a different.**

The Blues *loved* being **blue.**

They slurped **blueberry shakes**,
twanged **blue guitars**

and wore **blue bow ties.**

And *they* all agreed that being a **Blue** was
The. Best. Thing. Ever.

Problem was, the **Blues** didn't like the **Reds** _or_ the **Yellows.**

Now there was trouble!

And MORE trouble.

Keep your **red hats**
and **yellow bananas**
out of this area!

And EVEN MORE trouble!

until they all decided to
draw up some rules.

The Rules.

1. Only BLUES can walk in the BLUE area.

2. Nobody except <u>REDS</u> are allowed in the <u>RED</u> corner.

3. Stay away from bananas by order of the <u>YELLOWS</u>.

4. REDS, keep your hats to yourselves.

5. BLUES can only play in the RED corner if they give them some cheese.

6. No ball games!

7. Ok, some ball games if it's sunny.

8. No talking to each other.

9. No sharing.

10. No being friends!

The rules seemed to work for a while and all the differents were happy in their own space.

But then, quite unexpectedly . . .

along came **another** different.

And **another!**

I wish I had a red hat like yours.

I really like your glasses.

And another!

Then a really **different** different arrived.

The really **different** different liked **red apples, yellow bananas, blueberry shakes** and EVERY type of music.

And guess what?

Suddenly the rules didn't seem to matter anymore and everyone forgot about them.

The **differents** soon started to feel a lot happier. And finally they agreed on something . . .

Being **different** is the BEST THING EVER!